Weekly Reader Children's Book Club presents

THE BIG
CLEAN-UP

story and pictures by

HARVEY WEISS

Abelard-Schuman

London New York Toronto

© Copyright 1967, text and illustrations by Harvey Weiss
Library of Congress Catalogue Card Number: 67-13609
Printed in the United States of America
Weekly Reader Children's Book Club Edition

"What a mess!" said Peter's mother. They were standing in the doorway of Peter's room. They looked at the tangled bedclothes and the desk overflowing with odds and ends. The floor was littered with bits and pieces of broken toys and snippets and pippets and bits of this and that and other things.

"What a mess," said Peter's mother once again, shaking her head. "Where in the world does it all come from?"

"Gosh, I don't know," said Peter. "Do you think maybe it grows?"

"*You* don't know where it comes from, but *I* know where it is going. And that's OUT!" said his mother. "Go down to the basement and get two big cartons."

"Yes, m'am," said Peter.

His mother quickly made the bed. Then she
gathered everything into a big pile.
Peter came back with the boxes. His dog, Maurice—
a big, lazy, shaggy thing—was at his heels.
His mother said, "All right, now get to work.
Everything you don't need *throw out*. Put it in one
box. If there is anything you really *must* keep, put
it in the other box. And don't let Maurice nose
about."
"O.K.," said Peter. He sat down on the floor in
front of the large pile. Maurice scratched himself
a few times. He sniffed about a bit. Then he settled
down for a nap.

Peter picked up a crayon from the top of the pile.
He looked at it for a moment. "Well, I certainly
need this," he said, and he neatly printed on one of
the boxes: TO KEEP. On the other box he
lettered: TO THROW OUT.
"A very useful crayon," he said, and he dropped it
into the TO KEEP box.

He put a hand over his eyes. With the other he
reached in front. His hand closed on a long,
thin piece of wood.
Peter opened his eyes and examined the wood.
"It's too small," he said. "Out." He tossed it
into the TO THROW OUT box. "...Unless I wanted
to make something small?" He reached into the box,
took out the piece of wood and looked at it again.
"If it was a little longer I could make a bow
and arrow."

"Or it would make a good railing on a doghouse porch." He looked at Maurice who was curled up in a corner of the room fast asleep.

"One day...some day...I *am* going to build a doghouse for Maurice." Peter closed his eyes and thought about the sort of doghouse he would build. It would be large. So that Maurice could have friends come and visit him. It must have a porch, of course, and a big garage, a swimming pool, a helicopter landing deck on the roof and a lot of windows with white shutters.

Peter dropped the piece of porch railing into the TO KEEP box.

Peter saw a piece of cloth and pulled it out. He was ready to put it into the TO THROW OUT box, but, instead, he spread it out on the floor.

Then, he picked it up by two corners and waved it back and forth over his head. It looked nice.

"This has two uses," said Peter, and he listened carefully and thought he could hear the cheers of ten thousand people.

Then he heard the bull snorting. It lowered its
head and pawed the ground. The crowd fell silent—
waiting, tense and frightened.
Peter stood still, his feet slightly apart. Then the
bull charged! Peter leaned back, swinging
the cape in a graceful arc in front of the bull.

The bull's horns just grazed Peter, as it went
thundering by.
There was a great cheer and thunderous applause
and Peter turned and smiled at his fans. Then he
drew his sword and turned once more to face the bull....

"Or I could make a flag," thought Peter. He saw himself leading a hundred horsemen into battle, with the regimental banner flying overhead.

"That's what I'll do," he decided. "Some day
when I have the time I'll make a flag." He folded
the cloth neatly and placed it in the TO KEEP box.

Peter picked up an old rusty spark plug. He
imagined the noise of a small airplane engine.
Grmmmmmmmmmmm, phut, phut, pop…pop…
the engine stopped. There was silence except for the
sound of the air whistling by.
Peter took off his goggles and looked down.
The countryside spread out for miles and miles.
Forests and swamps and winding rivers baked in the
hot summer sun. No place to land.

"Oh dear," said Peter. He adjusted the controls
so that the plane was in a gliding position. Then
he climbed out of the cockpit and crawled forward
until he could reach the engine. He unscrewed one
of the spark plugs and tossed it away.
Reaching into his pocket, he took out the old
rusty spark plug. He cleaned it carefully and put
it in place. Then he worked his way back to the
cockpit and started up the engine. It purred
smoothly, and Peter thought, "How wise to have a
spare spark plug handy."
He dropped the old rusty spark plug in the
TO KEEP box.

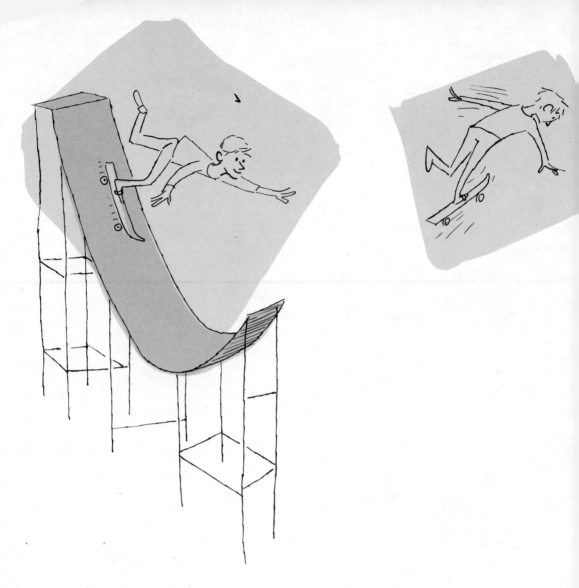

The pile was getting smaller now. Peter saw a
single roller skate and a single ski. He put the
ski on one foot and the roller skate on the other.
He shuffled about the room. Maurice opened one eye,
looked at Peter for a moment, and went back to
sleep.
"This isn't very good," said Peter. He took off
the ski and the skate. Then he suddenly realized what
he could do. He unbolted the skate, separating it
into two halves.

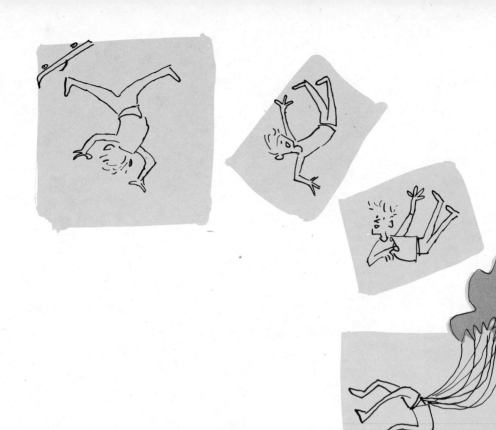

"I'll attach one half to the
front of the ski, and the other
half to the back of the ski.
That's what I'll do. I'll have
a *roller-ski!*" He gave the
skate wheels a twirl and dropped
them along with the ski in
the TO KEEP box.

Peter saw an empty spool.
"I have more than one of these," he said. He
poked around until he found several more. He piled
one on top of another. He tried lining them up end
to end. Then he placed them side by side.
"Seems a shame to throw them out," he said.
"Maybe I can invent something with them. How
about a dog wheelchair!" He looked through
the pile until he found a piece of paper and a
pencil. Then he sat down and drew his plans.

"If Maurice got a splinter in his foot and couldn't walk, he would certainly need a wheelchair like this. It's very practical. I'll have a factory and make thousands of them. I'll sell them for a great deal of money."

Peter leaned back and wondered just how many dog wheelchairs he could hope to sell. "It would probably depend on how many dogs get splinters in their paws," he decided.

He finished his plan for the dog wheelchair and folded it up. He found a rubber band and wrapped it around the spools and the plans and dropped it all into the TO KEEP box.

Peter saw something shiny. It was a magnifying lens with a chipped edge. "I'll use it in my new telescope," said Peter, as the doors in the roof of the observatory opened slowly.

"We are ready, professor," said the team of scientists.

Peter walked up to the telescope. He focused carefully. Then he took a long look.

Finally he stepped back and nodded to the scientists. "Gentlemen," he said. "Take a look. You'll see my discovery. A new planet. I shall name it *Peteroneus!*"

The scientists took turns looking through the telescope.

"Remarkable," said one.

"Incredible," said another.

"Pure genius," said the one with the longest beard.

And Peter smiled modestly in agreement as he dropped the chipped lens into the TO KEEP box.

Peter rummaged in the pile some more and found a piece of string. "For a kite," he decided. "I can't throw this away." Then he discovered a small cardboard box full of marbles. "Nobody throws out marbles," he said. And he said the same thing about a bag of smooth beach pebbles, a balloon, and a cigar box full of nuts and bolts.

He also decided that some day he might be able to fix the broken flashlight, the cracked hairbrush, the split plastic dump truck, the rusty alarm clock, the fountain pen without a point, the bicycle wheel, the compass without a needle, the boy scout knife with a broken blade and the portable radio that had been run over by a truck.

"Maybe all these things could be combined into something?" thought Peter. And he neatly placed all the objects in the TO KEEP box.

Now there was nothing left of the pile but three
old keys and a short piece of chain.
"You can never tell when you'll find a locked door,"
said Peter. "I'd better keep the keys."

Then he held up the chain and looked at it very carefully. "It's too small for a dog collar for Maurice," he said. He thought for a moment. "Of course. It's exactly the right size for an ostrich! I'll save it." And Peter placed it in the TO KEEP box. The pile was gone. The TO KEEP box was filled to the top.

Peter's mother walked in. "Good boy," she said.
"Let me have the box of junk you're throwing out
and I'll put it in the garbage."
"There's only one piece of junk to throw out,"
said Peter, "...this box. Here it is."
"You mean you're keeping everything?" said Peter's
mother.
"No, m'am. I'm throwing out the box."
"The *empty* box?"
"Yes, m'am," said Peter.
His mother sighed. "Oh well, all right. I'll get
rid of it." She picked it up and started to walk
out of the door.

"Wait a minute!" cried Peter. "You'd better let me keep the box. I think I'll cut a window in it and make a puppet stage."

So Peter took the empty TO THROW OUT box, and the filled-up TO KEEP box, and he put them both away in his closet.

THE END